AF373687

LOVE, LAUGH, *Lich*

Copyright © 2021 Kate Prior All rights reserved

The characters and events portrayed in this book are fictitious. Any similarity to real persons, living or dead, is coincidental and not intended by the author.

No part of this book may be reproduced, or stored in a retrieval system, or transmitted in any form or by any means, electronic, mechanical, photocopying, recording, or otherwise, without express written permission of the publisher.

ISBN: 9798847554268

Cover design by: Kate Prior
Printed in the United States of America

1

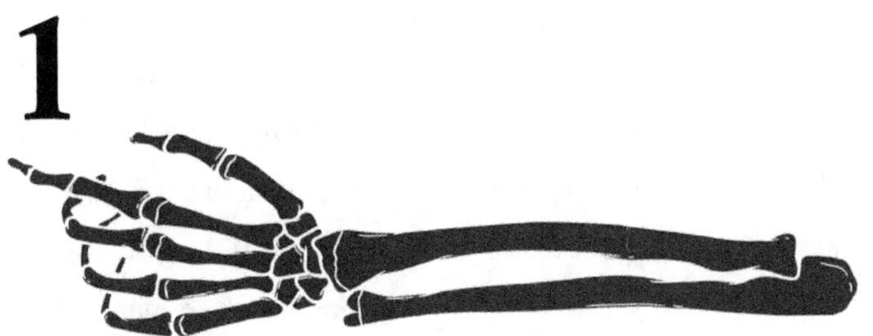

I never knew working at an office job would be this soul-sucking. I mean, everyone said it would be, and I expected some amount of sucking, but not like this.

It's one of those Tuesdays that feels a little too much like a second Monday. Specifically it feels like one of those Mondays that every little thing scratches against your consciousness like sandpaper on your face. The ticking of someone's watch. The creaky chairs that complain whenever someone shifts their weight a little. The smell of burnt coffee seeping out of the breakroom because putting the coffee pot directly beneath the drip is beyond some people.

I've never been an I-Hate-Mondays kind of person, but I think I might be turning into one, this very Tuesday.

It could just be because the washed out fluorescent lighting is giving me a headache. The conversation two cubicles over, the not-so-subtle whispering about vacation days, is making my eyes roll back in my skull. I can't focus on my spreadsheets. I'm not used to working with so many other people around. Maybe the reason I never contemplated hating my coworkers is because I wasn't with them for the whole day before. The only thing I'm capable of thinking about is how much I want to poke my head up over the divider and ask for some quiet.

Suddenly, I get my wish.

All the chatter silences, a sudden hush that feels heavy and old as a catacomb. A feeling like a breeze ripples through the room, as my skin prickles. An unnatural cold wraps around my body, when I see a dark shadow fall over me.

I look up into the hollow cowl of a black cloak that drapes down to the floor.

The spectre hangs near me with an empty stare that feels like standing on the edge of a cliff.

"Any messages, Lily?" the disembodied voice murmurs, low and guttural, coming from somewhere within the black robes that billow even without wind.

"I, uh, no, but I have a couple things people asked to reschedule," I stammer, shuffling through my desk for the little paper squares I've jotted down notes. I pause before I relay them to him, glancing around. I can see the color-drained faces of my coworkers peering out over their partitions to watch.

We usually do this in my office, but it's currently being renovated. I mean, I don't really have an office. I have a desk in the little waiting room outside the Dark Lich Lord's Grand Sanctum, where I sit and reschedule his appointments, remind him to take his daily blood doses, and really just tell people it'll be another ten minutes before they can see him.

At least, I used to have a desk. Until an assassin managed to sneak past security and tried to ambush the Lich Lord in the waiting room. It got messy. As in, pretty much all of the furniture was obliterated in the fight messy. I'd stepped away from my desk, only to return to a scorched room and a pile of cinders. Honestly, I don't even know why we have security if the Lich Lord can just vaporize anyone that comes at him with a poisoned blade.

There was a "chosen hero" or whatever a few years ago that tried to defeat the Lich Lord, but it didn't quite work out. There were details, but that kind of stuff gets buried in the endless paperwork that is required in maintaining an evil dominion. I don't think anyone has the real story except the Lich Lord himself.

Anyway, that's how I got stuck in one of the spare partitioned desks in the accounting department. It's only until the room is finished being renovated.

I glance over my shoulder and at the whole office still staring, unsubtly, to see what's going on.

It's right about then that I realize, most people in the Dark Domain don't get to see their Lich Lord all that often.

"Um, I'll bring these to the Sanctum, shall I?" I say, feeling their stares on my back.

Still, their stares are nothing compared to the gravity I feel when I look into the empty depth that is the Lich's cloak. The constant motion of his cloak is a slow, underwater-like movement that always makes me start to lean towards him. It's a weird, dizzying feeling. People talk about staring into the void until the void stares back, but that void is always staring.

The cloak's cowl nods stiffly, but the cold air of his presence feels more like an appreciative caress.

My chair makes an awful screech as I push it back against the floor; the sounds of me packing up my things from the desk are the only noises in the office. I dodge around a few desks and hurry after the Lich Lord to the Grand Sanctum.

Some people really haven't adjusted to life under the Dark Reign of Terror yet. Some things are different, but honestly it's all cosmetic. Things aren't that different from when we had a normal, living CEO.

And the thing about economic collapse and social upheaval is that there's a lot of room for upward mobility. At least that's what Janice from HR says, and I guess she's right, because I used to work in customer service, but now I'm a personal assistant to the Lich.

The Grand Sanctum is an utterly gorgeous room, once you get used to how creepy it is. It's about as big as a ballroom, but much more cluttered. The walls are lined with old bookshelves stuffed with dusty tomes and piled scrolls, occasionally featuring distilling glasses, crystals and jars of murky liquids. The windows are all stained glass in geometric patterns, all blue and green and purple. They don't let much light in, but they're my favorite part about stepping into the Dark Lord's office.

As the twenty-foot carved door shuts closed behind me, I start reading off the notes for today's schedule, the missives for him that I've sorted through by priority.

I get through maybe two of them before I realize the Dark Lord isn't listening in the slightest. Usually he interjects, making me take down notes about rearranging things or moving appointments up. I've never gotten this far without him at least canceling something.

He's pacing the lower inner level of the Sanctum, the ritual floor. It's drawn up in runes and incantation circles, with all his most-used ingredients lined up near the edges, and an altar for sacrifices in the center.

"…And there's that initiative to bring more women into STEM fields. That's Sneakiness, Traumatization, Evil Studies, and Misfortune," I trail off, watching his movement.

Definitely not listening.

"Is something the matter, Soven?" I ask. I don't usually use his first name, only when we're in his office together. I think it amuses him that he, an ageless entity with power beyond comprehension, is on a first name basis with a mortal like me. It's that social upheaval at work.

At that, the Dark Lord pauses in his pacing. He doesn't turn to look at me.

"Was it the assassination attempt?"

He gives a nod, and his cloak flutters like a sigh disturbs them. "Yes. I'm afraid it's left me somewhat unbalanced."

"It did cause quite a disruption. I've already briefed the legal department; they're working on how to deal with the agency that sent her. They've got some plans for a lawsuit, and some other options for how we should vet our outsourced labor in the future," I say.

That covers all the important concerns, but I wonder a bit if he hates having to seek me out at my new desk as much as I hate having to work there. After a moment I add, "I'm told the renovation should be finished in a few days."

He tilts his hood towards me in a way that feels reminiscent of a wry smile. "Sometimes I wonder who really is the Evil Overlord around here."

I contain a smile at the burst of pride. "I don't know what you mean," I say, shrugging, putting on a tone of utmost innocence.

"Well I didn't hire you for your looks," he starts to say, and cuts himself off. The cloak stiffens in something like a wince. "Not that I wouldn't. Or that there's anything wrong with your looks. They're very nice for a human. It's just not reign-policy to hire specifically on an appearance-basis-"

I smother a giggle behind my hand. "Quit while you're ahead."

Sometimes I really think the whole dark and ominous presence he exudes is just a front behind which he hides his social ineptitude. No one would exactly cower in terror at him if they knew he was kind of a dork.

The feeling of my smile fades as I watch him. If I thought there were shoulders under that cloak of perpetual billowing, I would have thought they'd sunk down in frustration.

"I'm at a loss, Lily," he says, the cloak's hood turning to look deep into one of the greenish fires. "For how to complete this ritual."

My eyes fall to the ritual circle. Now that he brings it up, it does look about the same as I saw it arranged last week. Usually things get moved around, new symbols drawn on it, etc.

"If you need me to order more ingredients, I can take down a list," I begin, wondering where I'm going to get a copy of the requisition forms when my usual desk is now ash.

But Soven shakes his head.

"There are many magical things that can't be collected in vials," Soven explains. "A last breath. A first kiss. A shiver over the skin."

I fall silent, his words provoking my imagination. I don't know much about magic, and he's never told me much about how he does what he does.

"Last week, the woman who was in the waiting room, before I—" he jerks his head and makes a clicking noise with his teeth, referring back to the vaporization event, "But these assassins are becoming craftier by the day, they must have infiltrated that agency. There's no knowing who I can trust, now."

I nod. Initially, we had hired the woman through an agency, had her vetted for her services through them. I hadn't really known what services exactly she was supposed to provide at the time, and when my brain puts two together, I nearly laugh.

"Hang on, is that what you needed? A shiver?" I ask skeptically. "That's what we're outsourcing for?"

The cloak's hood turns slowly to me, and he nods.

I'm doing my best to keep my face straight. I let out a quiet laugh as I say, "You could have just called me in. I've got skin."

I wonder if that last remark is rude or something. After all, he doesn't really have skin, to my knowledge. I hope I don't have to take an undead sensitivity training class now.

The cloak's hood stares through me for a few long, uncomfortable moments. The air doesn't grow colder, instead I'm too warm about the collar, and maybe it's not anything supernatural, my face is reddening under the intensity of his attention.

Every second in the hourglass slipping by makes me think my suggestion was perhaps really dumb. I don't know, maybe he needed a professional to shiver for him. Maybe professionally rendered shivers are higher quality? I've never really thought about it before.

"You do," he notes, something different in his voice. He's looking at me, and I don't think he's ever stared at me this long.

Is he looking at my skin? Everything that isn't covered by my office clothes, my arms and shins and my collar, all of it feels oddly on display. I fight the urge to cross my arms over myself or any other way of covering myself up.

"You do," he repeats, crossing the Sanctum towards me, less like he's moving towards me, more like the room is shrinking the space between us. With him comes that scent of herbs, a heavy dose of clove, thyme, lavender, cedar, and a slight hint of embalming fluids.

"Yeah, I do," I echo, my voice nearly a whisper and more than enough for how close we are. Either I feel like I'm underwater with him or I feel that I'm in over my head. Maybe I'm not as used to being in my boss's presence as I think I am, because by now I'd usually have gone back to my little not-a-real-office.

He towers over me, staring into my soul probably. I mean, as far as I can tell, the cloak's hood doesn't have eyeballs, but even as I look into that endless void, I can feel his gaze sweeping over me, sending goosebumps over my skin.

His head tilts ever so slightly, like he can tell.

When my coworkers talk about the chills Soven gives them, it's all 'frailty of life' this, and 'acute sense of my mortality' that.

And for an undying Lord of Darkness, that makes sense.

But when he looks at me, I get this feeling like walking through an old house, where all the furniture has sheets draped over them while the house is dormant, and suddenly, someone is dragging the sheets off. Like he's unveiling me; like plucking petals off a flower, to see what's hiding at the center.

"You would really do that," he says, unconvinced. He makes it sound like I'm chopping off an arm.

"Shiver-rly isn't dead yet," I say, trying a wide smile. It feels like the best thought I've had today, until I hear myself say it and wince. I cough. "Uh. Yeah. It's no big deal."

He's still for a long moment, before he nods. He tilts his head to the ritual floor. "Come then."

It's then, creeping down into the ritual floor, careful not to step on any of the lines, that I realize I've never been so far into this room. Maybe I'm too used to being able to duck back out the door as soon as I'm done.

Standing by the Sanctum doors, hugging the walls, is an entirely different experience from crossing to the middle, which borders on agoraphobic. I've never needed the closeness of my flimsy cubicle walls so much. The sound of my breath echoes off the tiles, the only sound in the hall, making me feel like I should maybe hold my breath. My footsteps against the marble punctuate the air so loud I nearly wince with each one.

I hike my skirt up a bit as I hop onto the altar Soven gestures to, straightening it as I sit down and lay back.

The stone is cold to touch, and there's something about laying across this ledge in the center of the room that makes me feel more than exposed. How can I feel practically naked with all my clothes still on?

Maybe it's the giant mirror on the ceiling.

It's pretty high up, but I can see myself, wavy brown hair spread around me, the lush dark green of my skirt. It's too far away to see my freckles or birthmarks, or the buttons on my blouse.

Oh shit, I think my nipples are hard because it's so damn cold in the ritual space. I try to inconspicuously crane my head up for a better look to check if they're visible through my blouse.

"Everything all right?" Soven asks, crossing to my side.

"Yes!" I squeak, a little too quickly. Ugh.

His voice is deeper than the abyss. When he talks to me, sometimes his words reverberate down my body and find all my hollow spaces. Too often I find it's left me biting my lip.

It's hard for me to believe there's absolutely nothing under that cloak. There's gotta be at least bones or something. I speculated as much to Janice from HR once, and she laughed, "Why, so you can jump those bones?"

Suffice it to say, I haven't told anyone about what his voice does to me or my thoughts about what he really looks like. I pretend not to think about my undead boss in any unprofessional way.

"Just lay back and relax," he intones, like he's used to doing this. He must be, he's done probably hundreds of rituals, and this is my first. "Close your eyes."

There is something soothing in the way he flips through pages of his tomes, muttering incantations as he sprinkles herbs and splashes of potions into the cold burning fire.

As soothing as listening to him move about is, I can't help but feel the moments stretch thin with curiosity and anticipation. I wonder how he's going to make me shiver. I'd think the easiest way would be to turn the thermostat way down, but he seems to have a more arcane approach.

I almost startle out of my skin when his touch ghosts down my bare shoulder. A whisper crawls up my neck, and I feel something soft, something almost like skin with a light down of fur over it. It's like the soft side of cured leather, but alive.

I shiver alright. I shiver right down to my godsdamnned vagina, that moth-wing flutter low in my belly as my clit pulses awake with interest. The need for him to drag that touch, mouth or whatever it is, over more of my body is so visceral, I nearly moan.

If he couldn't tell my nipples were hard through my bra before, I'm almost absolutely sure he can now.

I can feel the magic buzzing in the air as the last ingredient completes the ritual, but I keep my eyes squeezed shut. I've seen the light blaze from under the door when he's done rituals before.

The air abates, and after a few minutes I hope it's safe enough to peek around. When I look up again, his attention is buried back in his books, as he scribbles something down.

I guess he doesn't need me now, and I should probably get back to work.

Still, I pause when I get to the door, glancing back at him.

"...I've never been kissed, either," I say after a moment.

It's true. A few years ago, a fortune teller told me that my soulmate was the champion who would overthrow the Dark Reign. And I, a naïve dummy at the time, believed her. I should have seen then that it was a load of crock to get me to waste more money on her tarot booth, but it kept me saving that kiss for the chosen one. By the time there were rumors of his death, I'd realized what a fool I'd been. It was hard to get close to anybody at that, when the takeover and acquisition happened, there was so much chaos. After that, well, I was too busy being Soven's personal assistant.

I feel foolish saying it, not because I'm ashamed of being a virgin or whatever, but because who says that to her boss?

I duck out the door before he can say anything, before he can see the way my cheeks turn red, and hopefully before he realizes how much I want him to be that first kiss.

2

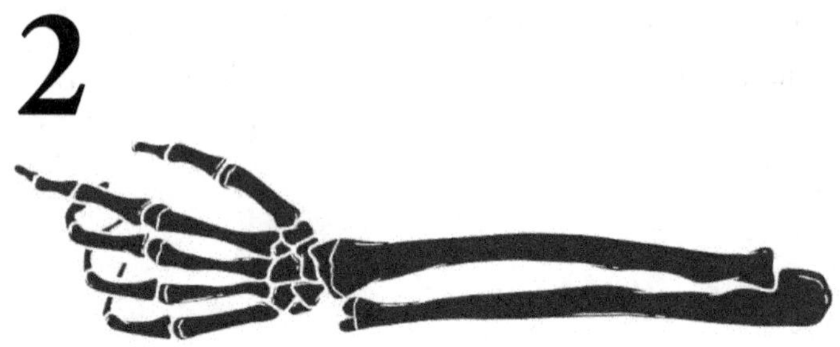

"I mean, there's no ethical consumption under evil dominion," I sigh, rolling my eyes at Janice from HR. "The 'organic' label doesn't mean it's better, it just means it's more expensive."

The intern had come around to get everyone's coffee run orders, and Janice has a problem with decaf tea made with orphan tears.

Janice huffs. "They wouldn't need to make a distinction between organic and non-organic if there wasn't a difference."

"Look, I'm not going to argue, it's not for me, it's for Sov— the Dark Lord. I don't want to just swap something out, what if there's a, like, dietary reason he needs it?"

Janice rolls her eyes, and doesn't try to refute that. We've had this conversation a dozen times. Sometimes I think she likes being difficult.

Janice heads back to her office and I add my own coffee order to the intern's list. I used to be able to keep up with the names, but it feels like there's a new one every week.

Turnover is pretty quick around here; a lot of people do get sacrificed. Pentagram, candles, chanting, the whole shebang. We used to have little going-away parties whenever that happened, but there have been budget cuts. At least the severance package is good.

When the Dark Reign first started here, there were a lot of staff cuts. I was on the chopping block, so to speak. As I understand it, a number of virgin sacrifices had to be made to increase his power.

It's so funny to think of what things were like then, compared to now. I'd been tied up to the rack, The Dark Lord had come in, let me tell you, he had been the picture of an unhappy customer, mostly because of the company's slipshod record keeping. Lucky for me, I was an expert in dealing with unhappy clients.

He'd given me a chance that day to prove myself, and though every day he'd say this was the day he'd finally sacrifice me, every day I'd prove useful with managing things. I think I can pinpoint the moment he decided to keep me close by-- I went into his office to drop off some internal reports about an hour before he realized he even needed them.

It's almost an hour later when the intern returns and makes the rounds to everyone's desks, getting to me last because he forgot my office-slash-waiting-room had been obliterated and he couldn't find my borrowed cubicle.

As soon as he sets the cups down on my desk I snatch them up, hurrying down the carpeted hallway.

I don't like being late with anything, and that's my main focus as I push through the Dark Sanctum's doors without knocking, announcing as I come in, "Tea's here!"

As soon as the words leave my mouth, I can see that I definitely should have knocked.

It hadn't occurred to me that there would be anything resembling a body under that cloak. Honestly I thought at most he was made of maybe just bones under there, if anything at all, from the way his cloak always flutters weightlessly like it really is only a piece of fabric in the wind.

But he shrugs off the cloak, and he has a body.

A body that couldn't possibly fit underneath it without magic. He shrugs it off, distorting the rules of physics like fitting a table under a handkerchief.

He's definitely more than bones. Out of his cloak, he's broad shouldered and broad-chested and really just broad in every direction. My mind has a hard time grasping how the cloak could have made his body disappear into almost nothing, when his body is so much…everything.

His legs have an animal shape to them, the way you can't really tell what's supposed to be the knees on a deer's back legs. But maybe that's because I don't spend a lot of time looking for his knees, rather the shape of his ass before his tail interrupts it.

And my heart stops, like the ground falling out from under me, when he realizes the door is open and turns around.

His face is almost lion-like, or maybe it's bear-like and I'm just thinking about lions because of the sheer volume of his mane of— hair? Fur? The rack of four large horns?

The hair continues in a war path down his stupidly broad chest, my eyes drag across a still broad, toned, leathery torso, and stop short after his hips. Yeah, why would a Dark Lord have any need for pants?

I don't know what to make of what I see, but that's not like any human penis I've ever seen. Or any kind, really. There's a lot going on there, and I'm half caught between a warm spike of curiosity to explore and the sheer confusion of why on earth there would be so many.

"OH MY GODS, I'm so sorry," I blurt out and duck back out the door. Oh my gods, my gods, I'm so fired.

I swallow and open the door again just enough to stick the tea inside on the nearest ledge, and flee.

I want to crawl under my desk. I end up pacing back and forth in front of Janice's office for a while, trying to think of what I'd even say to her. I don't know what I'd even ask her for, maybe some reassurance that I can't be sacrificed for walking in on the wrong moment?

I walk down the wrong hallway two, maybe three times, I'm so distracted with the aftershock images of the sheer broadness of all that I've witnessed. It's kind of a big change to go from wondering about my boss's lack of body to his one hell of a body.

Eventually, I go back to my temporary desk and bury myself in paperwork. The handful of times I would have normally poked my head into Soven's office to deliver messages and remind him of appointments, I chicken out and talk the intern into dropping the messages off.

I think I spend the next few hours repeatedly burying my face in my hands, on and off. Every so often, my mind sneaks back to what I saw, and more importantly, what I'm not quite sure I saw. I don't know what I expected to be in an immortal Lich's lack of pants, but it wasn't multiple appendages.

I need therapy to bury the image of my boss's junk deep into the unused parts of my brain. Maybe hypnotherapy. I take an hour or so flitting around the HR department, looking for information to see if the employee health plan covers that.

The end of the work day nears, eventually. People gather up their cloaks and head out into the miasma, saying their goodnights.

"Working late?" Randall from accounting asks as he passes my temporary desk on his way out.

"Just catching up on some things," I lie. I've been watching the hallway to the Dark Sanctum from my position like a hawk. Randall says something encouraging sounding on his way out, I don't really catch it.

If the Dark Lord's not going to fire me, maybe I'll apologize for not knocking, and hope that puts an end to it. I can't get any work done if I'm all wrapped up in my own embarrassment.

Eventually I summon the courage to approach the door, and then a few minutes later, knock, wait, and open it.

My gaze inches carefully around the room, and for some reason, I'm surprised to see him back in his cloak, a normal-sized floating specter once more, pouring over his spell books.

"Did you get my note to clear tomorrow's appointments?" he asks without looking up.

"I—yes, the intern brought it by. I've rescheduled most of them," I confirm.

"Very good."

There's a note of tired dismissal in his voice. When I hear that I usually ask if that will be all for tonight, and leave him to his experiments. But I don't move. I can't. I can't just ignore what happened this morning.

I try to apologize. Those aren't the words that happen, though.

"I--I was just checking in to see if you needed anything for your rituals before I left for the day, shivers or sneezes or whatever," I blabber on, and nearly kick myself for doing so. Somehow saying that seemed less embarrassing than 'Sorry I saw your dick, er, dicks, sir'.

The head of his cloak turns to look at me, as he straightens up. "…Well, nothing that's set up for, currently. I've put all those rituals off until I can sort out this assassin issue."

I nod. That makes sense.

At least things seem normal between us. Maybe nudity isn't an issue when you're undying. Maybe I can come into the office tomorrow and pretend it didn't happen.

I'm on the precipice of leaving, when he turns his head back to his books, flipping through them.

"Actually, there is something that would be helpful," he says, glancing back up. He lifts a heavy tome, flipping through pages of diagrams. "There is a spell that would help me locate how the assassins are getting in."

I wait, fidgeting with my fingers behind my back as he scans page after page. I take a few steps further into the room, peering around. There's broken glass on the floor by a window, newly boarded up.

He barely looks up as he says, "I need to trap the essence of a first kiss in this ritual field, so I can distill it down to the vulnerability of the act."

A kiss. I've daydreamed a couple of times about standing on my toes and poking my face into that dark, seemingly empty cowl of his, to see if I could taste that darkness. I don't know if that counts as thinking about kissing my boss, because I didn't know he had a real, tangible mouth until this morning. And I wasn't really preoccupied with the face part at all this morning, considering what else I saw.

"Well. I've never, uh, been first kissed, so," I nod quickly, a touch too eagerly. Foot, mouth, thoroughly acquainted. I'm digging my own grave while standing in quicksand. I don't think it matters at this point. "That works."

Soven gestures with a wave of his black cloak to the shelves, and a number of vials float off the shelves to the ritual floor, starting the preparation.

Then I see his hands, his real hands, come out from within the cloak, moving to take it off. The hood turns to me, and I realize he wants me to turn around. I do so quickly, swallowing. If my heart rate picks up again at the thought of him out of that magic cloak again, well hopefully he can't tell from across the room.

I wait, averting my eyes as he sheds the cloak again, and by the sound of it, finds some cloth to wrap around his lower half like a grand, draped towel. When I hear him prowling around the room freely, the weight of his footsteps approaching me, I take a deep breath and carefully lift my gaze.

A beast. A few years ago I never gave much thought to what a Lich was, but the powerful form before me begs as many new questions as it answers. The only one that presses on my tongue, however: *does anyone else know?*

His eyes are molten gold, and burning into me. I shiver with that feeling of slowly being exposed, layers of coverings peeled back until I'm nothing but my skin and my rapid pulse.

My gaze still dips down once the loincloth's in place, and instantly bounces back up to his horns. I bite down on my lips to avoid making any kind of face in reaction, but my mind is running with the sparse glance I had this morning and the size of the bulge through the sheet.

"Ok. So," I say, matter-of-factly and as business-like as possible. In an attempt to not to look down again, I try to think about spreadsheets. I need to replace my unprofessional thoughts with professional ones. It's as I'm staring hard at his face, the gravity of the moment sinks in.

Oh, no, what do I do with my hands? Should they be this clammy?

I shake it off as best I can. It's just a kiss. It's not like the first one is particularly important to me, I just never happened to get around to it. It's not like a big, romantic thing to me. It doesn't matter where I waste it.

I put my hands on his chest, and push up on my tiptoes, I'm ripping the bandage off, and getting this done.

My mouth meets Soven's without ceremony. It's softer than I expected, and that catches me off guard enough to not immediately pull away.

The sharp teeth that jut from his jaws nip gently at my lower lip. We've never been so close before, and nose to nose, there's no guise of mystery when I can feel so much of him against me. I feel like I know him better just by being able to touch him. I can feel his careful intent in the way he moves his mouth against mine with purposeful kisses, the fleeting brush of his tongue to my teeth before I mirror the action.

The longer it goes on, the more I hope it never ends, the more I want from this. I push into the kiss, dragging my teeth along his lip.

My hands are digging into his leathery flesh, grasping for more of him until they're gripping handfuls of his mane. As I start to slip from my precarious balance on my toes—I really needed a step stool for this—a large clawed hand curls around the low of my back, pressing me up into his body, holding me steady. My feet leave the floor and I think I lose a shoe, but

I'm fighting the instinct to put my hands around his horns and wrap my legs around his waist. I'm fighting that need and, I think, losing as I feel the bulge in the sheet press against my thighs. I find my hand pushing down on his shoulder to bring me up, some shadow of a thought to grind my hips to his. His mouth leaves mine and I feel the scrape of his teeth against my neck.

I gasp, and that's the sound that breaks this.

It seems to rouse him from our kiss, and he pulls back to his full height, setting me back down, my shoe-less foot touching the cold tile again. His claws rest loosely around my back, caging me in.

His shoulders are like a fireplace mantel, taking ragged, heaving breaths, I realize I'm breathing heavily too.

"So, um, was that what you needed?" I pant. It was what I needed, but I think I might need more in a minute.

Soven's molten gaze lingers on me a moment, before his eyes flick to the right. "…The ritual floor is over there."

"…Oh," I say. Oh. My cheeks warm. "You wouldn't happen to need any more virgin sacrifices, would you?"

3

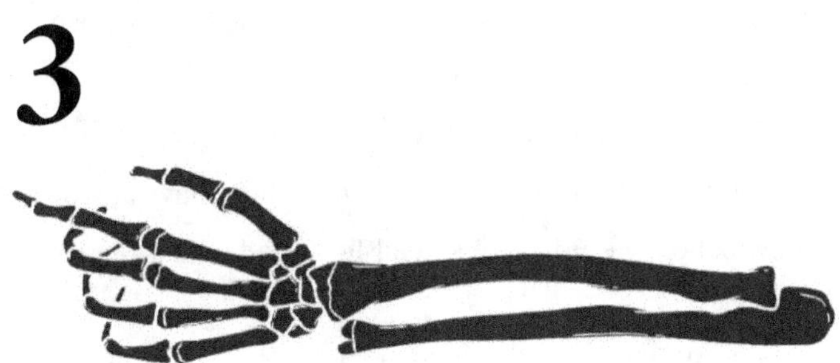

There's flowers on my desk when I arrive the next morning.

I sit down, marveling at the size of the bouquet. It takes up perhaps three-fourths of my desk. It's hundreds of lily of the valley stems, slender curved hooks of bell-like flowers, mixed with sprigs of rosemary. It perfumes the whole office.

'For your efforts', the card reads in Soven's handwriting, and I'm sure my face turns scarlet.

That's one way to refer to the fact I totally mistimed the kiss.

"Secret admirer?" Randall from Accounting asks, noting the flowers. He's the first to arrive in the accounting department this morning, after me. He waggles his eyebrows teasingly. He's nice, and he's been helpful the last couple days I've been working next to him.

"No. No, um, just a thank-you, from uh, a client," I lie badly, and hope Randall doesn't realize I don't have any of my own clients, I just make spreadsheets and take office inventory.

"Oh. Well, that's nice of them," he nods, and settles into his cubicle across from me. "Hey, um, have you ever thought about switching to accounting? Or, uh, some other department. It doesn't have to be this one."

"Stay in accounting?" I ask, confused. I raise an eyebrow at Randall. "But I like my job the way it is."

Randall backpedals instantly.

"I mean, it's nice being able to talk to you, instead of just waving through the waiting room window," he says, cheeks turning red as he starts to ramble himself into a corner. I let the conversation peter out.

I try to stick the massive mound of flowers under my borrowed desk, it only partially works. I can't really get any work done with it on top, though.

The flowers bother me in a weird way. Not that Soven sent them. The fact that he did makes my heart do weird fluttery things, and my brain leads down a trail of thoughts that ends with me pressing my knees harder together. I kind of wish I'd let myself grind fully against him, thinking that a little more friction would have satisfied my curiosity. He was so gentle to kiss, so careful in how he held me, I feel like he would have let me do almost anything.

The thing that bothers me is the card. It sort of strikes through all the fluttery feelings, like they're meant to be a get-well-soon bouquet and not a thanks-for-the-very-hot-kiss gift.

Besides, *I'm* the personal assistant. Who else would he have told to order the flowers? Does he have a second personal assistant somewhere? I don't believe he knows how to locate a florist by himself.

All this thinking about my weird little crush and that kiss is distracting me from my work though. All I've done in the last five minutes is doodle hearts and 'Mrs. Lich' on my post-its.

I'm going to shove down the want to see him out of his cloak again. There will be no more offering shivers or first kisses to his rituals.

"Uh, Lily?"

I whirl around and maybe glare a little too much at the intern, who shrinks back instantly.

"Um, yes?" I shake myself, trying to show a kinder face to him.

The intern's shoulders loosen a touch. "Um, Mr. Dark Lord told me I was to-- um. Help you out. With your workload?"

My brow furrows and I frown reflexively. "Why would I need help?"

The intern makes a helpless face and shrugs at me. "It's what I was told. I can uh, do the spreadsheets and inventory stuff? I did that at my old job."

I stare at the intern, uncomprehending. That's my work. The stuff I do. With the exceptionally neat lines and color-coded charts that make me feel at peace with the world. And I'm supposed to what, delegate it?

"You can sort through incoming mail and prioritize it," I say, instead of 'No, go back to whatever department you're actually interning in'.

Half of my irritated mood is fueled by the fact I'm sharing half of my work with the intern and the other half is that I suddenly have all the time in the world to let my mind wander. What, one flubbed kiss and suddenly Soven thinks I can't do my job?

An hour later, I'm *not* thinking about whether he needs to send out to an agency for another first kiss, one he can actually use for his spells. I'm *not* snapping my quills in half in jealousy at the thought of some stranger getting to see him without his cloak, seeing the real Soven, *kissing* the real Soven—

The sound of a snap turns three of the nearest heads in neighboring cubicles towards me, including Randall. He gives me a slightly concerned look.

I look down and see that I have broken another quill, and ripped through the paper with it.

Ok, maybe I have been snapping quills in some kind of mood, but it's not a jealous one.

Eventually, mostly to get away from my new desk buddy, I bring in the daily tea, and find Soven sitting at his desk. I do glance around, making sure there isn't some secondary personal assistant, or worse, a personal assistant that I'm secondary to. When there isn't one, I cross the Sanctum and round the desk to his side, setting the tea down.

"I got your flowers," I say, not letting my frustration color my tone. "They're lovely."

He gives me a curt nod. I itch to touch him, to try to rekindle that brief connection from yesterday. I can't stand the little space between us, the way I can't discern the feelings under his reactions.

I chew my tongue and try to think how I'm going to bring up my issue with suddenly being saddled with the intern. I can't tell how receptive he'll be.

He's not in the cloak. Something about that makes me warm. He's got the loincloth wrapped around his middle, though. I craned my neck a little because of the way he's sitting, knees spread far apart, leaning far back. The stack of papers in his inbox never seems to decrease as he plucks one off the top, makes a notation or signature, and puts it in one of the outgoing boxes.

After a moment, he notices the cup of tea I've brought in for him, and he puts aside his quill.

"I don't know what I would do without you," he sighs, leaning back in his chair. "Probably the whole Dark Reign would fall apart."

Like that, all my frustration is extinguished with the sheer validation and appreciation in those words. My heart feels all wobbly and softened, possibly dizzy from the whiplash of my own emotions.

There's something about standing so near him, the ease between us. Looking upon him however, makes my body stir, my heart beat faster, heat move low in my stomach.

He looks over to me and gives me a smile, and suddenly my chest aches with feeling.

It's never going to go back to how it was before, I realize with a swallow. We've broken a boundary that can't be rebuilt, whether it was that kiss, that glimpse, or that shiver. Maybe all of them together. I've wandered too far into the way his presence affects me, and I can't imagine pretending to be satisfied with less of it than I've managed to steal so far.

I'm staring at the altar in the center of the ritual floor, thinking about how it made me feel to sit there. A hazy thought comes to mind, and before I can consider all its faults, I voice it.

"Is there any other way you can… trap the essence of vulnerability, or whatever?"

My question pauses the Dark Lord in his work.

"Any other true act of vulnerability," he shrugs after a moment, the answer like a component to an alchemical equation.

"I'm sorry I messed up, and wasted the first kiss yesterday," I say, feeling that wholeheartedly. I hadn't realized what I'd been feeling then, and I'd blundered on through because I couldn't make sense of it. But I understand myself better now. I know what I'm craving, and I know it won't end on its own. "Would you let me try again?"

My declaration is met with hesitation. Soven turns his eyes on me, assessing me as his gaze sweeps up and down.

"I value the loyalty you've shown me," he murmurs at long last, his answer one of utmost diplomacy. "But I would not ask to overstay your generosity."

The formality of his words nearly bruises me, but I catch the interest in his eye, the patient waiting in his expression.

He knows he can't ask anything more of me. He knows anything he asks of anyone will always be met with resounding choruses of 'Yes, my lord', bowing and scraping included.

Anything to do with me, it has to be given freely. I chew my bottom lip, my determination setting in.

"My Dark Lord," I say, holding his golden gaze. "I always fix my mistakes."

He gazes back at me, curiosity setting in.

With a flick of his fingers, the ritual floor lights anew, ready for me.

I cross the sanctum to sit on the altar, but unlike before, I don't lay back. My skin feels tingly just being here, and I know it's the magic of the circle, mixing with my own nerves. If I hesitate at all, I'll lose my nerve.

My fingers go to buttons on my blouse, undoing them with the practice of habit. Once all the buttons are open, I slip my blouse and skirt off, leaving me in only my underwear.

There's the scratch of his chair against the floor as he pushes out from his desk, standing. He crosses to the edge of the ritual floor, but stays outside the boundaries of it.

The way he moves is lined with caution, but he doesn't disguise the hunger in his eyes.

When I shrug off my last layers, standing naked before the altar, I watch him pace the outer edge of the circle, feeling his stare, the way it strips me down beyond bare, the palpable want.

I see the way the runes don't change. They don't react the way they did when I gave Soven that shiver, and I know it's because this isn't true vulnerability. The act of standing naked doesn't put enough on the line, but what I'm about to do will.

"I have a confession," I say, swallowing. The thoughts I don't bring to work with me, the ones I tuck under my tongue when I'm in the office. The ones that have been piling up in my mind, demanding to be let out.

"Don't tell me you're another assassin," he says, though amusement curls his lip.

I'd smile back if I wasn't so nervous.

I sit down on the stone altar, leaning back on one arm. I try not to make eye contact with the giant mirror above me. If I look at it, I feel like it'll show me the things I don't want to see. I can't think about any of the ways this could be a mistake, or I'll stop.

I draw a finger up my breast, toying with the hardened nipple. "Ever since that shiver, I've been having dreams about you."

I lick my lips, watching the twitch of his cocks under his loincloth give away his interest. Even with his hand casually draped over the knot of the sheet, concealing part of himself, the evidence of his arousal is plain.

"Dreams?" he near growls, the sound sending a pulse of want between my legs. I nod, unable to look at him.

"Dreams that leave me aching and craving you when I wake up," I continue. I can feel the magic swelling around me as I confess each word. "Dreams where that kiss didn't stop."

I hesitate a moment, before I lay back against the altar, spreading my knees far apart enough that my hands can go between my legs that I can touch myself before him.

I pause, my eyes on the way his gaze falls to my cunt. I trace the slick wetness up the outer edges of my folds. I feel almost powerful, the way his stare is trained on my hand, even when I take my hand up to taste myself off my fingertips. The guttural noise he makes in response makes my hips twitch.

I bite back my smile, before passing my fingers down over my clit. There's a shock of pleasure when I finally rub myself, a prickling on my skin from the magic. I've never been watched like this before, never so openly and brazenly.

"I want you to use me," I gasp, stroking my clit with one hand. I look at his arousal still covered by the towel, the way he palms his cocks through it. Looking at it, I know the fingers I'm curling into myself can't possibly compare. It doesn't do nearly enough to sate the aching want of my cunt.

"Need me," I beg, knowing I'm giving too much of myself away with those words. "Need more of me. Use me, to whatever end."

It's far too soon when the magic takes what it needs, stealing the essence it needs. The candles blaze a moment, and burn themselves out.

The runes go dark, and then it's only me and Soven, our gazes locked.

He holds me in his stare for a long, calculating moment. His loincloth falls aside, revealing his hard, leaking cocks. "I shall."

4

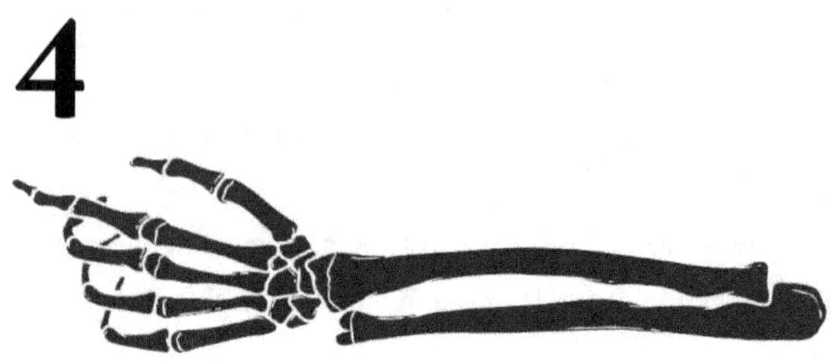

I swallow, watching Soven stand across the ritual circle, half wreathed in the precipice of shadow. The room is dark and smoky from the last ritual, and all I can see is within the faint light of the stained glass windows.

Soven approaches, the heavy sound of his footfalls timed with each needy pulse of my cunt. I've laid myself bare for this beast, and I think I might give everything of myself to him, I'm sick with want. The magic gives a heady buzz to the air, and I feel like I have to breathe heavier just to stay upright.

He waves, making a gesture that sends vials of tinctures floating across the room to set up a new ritual, but I have no eyes for the inanimate objects doing his bidding.

I sit up to see all of him standing before me. He's shed his loincloth, and now that I'm directly eye level with his strange cocks, I still don't really know what to make of them, but the longer I look the more I find myself toying with my bottom lip in interest.

It seems kind of three-pronged. The middle cock seems to be the longest, most actually cock-like of the three, though the head is shaped differently, rounder, with little ridges patterning down the shaft.

The one on top seems to be less of a cock and more like a… something. It too looks different at the tip, a sort of puckered shape, a wet sheen glistening over it. The one at the bottom concerns me a little because it's almost as long as the middle cock, though not nearly as girthy.

I swallow, dragging my eyes up to his. He's been watching me, assessing, waiting to see if my plea holds up, now that I can see what I'm in for.

My breath grows ragged as I summon what steadfastness I can, and nod.

Soven huffs a breath, rolling his shoulders in response before he kneels before me. He pulls my knees apart, exposing my cunt to open view.

He takes in the sight of me like that for a long moment, before he drags a finger with its blunted claw carefully up through my folds and I whimper at the touch. I'm not scared that he's going to hurt me, he's too precise for that to happen. It's the anticipation I don't know if I can live through. My whole body is on edge, tightly wound up in arousal, waiting for how he'll use me.

He dips his head down, and I can feel his hot breath ghost over my cunt, the graze of his mouth barely against me. The first lick of his tongue is a revelation, textured with little bumps that are a cascade of stimulation, making my back coming up off the dais.

He puts one clawed hand on my ribs, so large it spans up to my breast. He holds me in place, the pad of his thumb teasing my nipple.

His tongue is long and hot dragging through my folds, each tortuously awaited flick over my clit making me quiver.

Every few strokes he snakes that tongue up inside me, lapping greedily at my wetness, filling me blissfully, giving brief relief to my aching walls. It's all I can do to keep my hips from bucking against his face. My hands bury in his mane to keep him over my clit, and he covers one of my hands with his to encourage me— to guide him, to hold his horns while I grind, and roll my hips against his face.

I squirt before I reach my climax, the liquid scattering around my legs in droplets as he continues to lick me through it, not missing a beat. I make some ungodly noises, and soon his licking slows and he pulls back. I whimper when he stops, wanting more.

"Keep doing that, please," I beg. He doesn't even have to fuck me, if he only does that forever, I'll be happy.

He gives my cunt one last, tortuous lick that leaves me quivering, wanting that release that had begun to build once more, fading with the seconds that slip past, when he stands again, gives his cocks a few readying jerks. It's then I realize his tongue had been preparing me for this.

He slips the middle cock in my cunt, easing in. He's thick, stretching me to my limits. He pulls back a couple inches, feeding me little by little. He toys with my folds again, finding my clit, over sensitive from all the licking. I let out a cry of surprise at the feeling of the sucker of his top cock pressing to it.

He chuckles, a deep throaty noise that rumbles through his chest. He shifts his hips, easing into me further, and that's when I encounter the third cock, the way its thin shaft slides through the narrow gap of my ass cheeks, grazing against my hole. It doesn't penetrate me, but it teases both the idea and the skin.

I swear, when he pushes in all the way to the hilt, he's so far up he's gotta be hitting other organs. At least, that's what it feels like. His body tenses up, and he lets out a low groan. He takes my hips in his hands, starting to truly thrust. The top cock's suckers begin working faster, sucking and popping against my clit.

By some miracle I don't come immediately, and I savor each thrust harder, each suck and near-breech of my asshole, the way he's licking my tits. Each time he pulls back, I want to whimper at the feeling of how empty it feels, only to have the breath nearly knocked out of my chest when he ruts back into me.

The relentless sweet friction of it builds against the tension curling in me, his thrusting quickening until I cannot feel his absence. There is only him pounding into me, his hands digging into my ass, his mouth dragging against my nipples. I get lost in the sensation of it, losing all semblance of time or space until I come hard.

I'm not sure if the orgasm lasts forever, or if it just feels like it. Every shudder is compounded by his thrusts, the way he keeping fucking me open even after I'm spent, every pleasure-raw nerve being dragged back into another climax.

The second orgasm makes me feel like the first one wasn't even important. I'm clenching around him, and I languish in the sudden slickness of him coming in me, the way my orgasm coaxes his, dragging out each spurt of come, until he collapses and rolls me over on top of him, his center cock still twitching inside me, the sticky mess dripping out slowly.

Exhaustion lays heavy over my entire body, a sheen of sweat covers my skin. I'm strewn limp, collapsed over Soven's body, like he's my own personal mattress instead of me being his fuck toy. His hand is heavy against me, claws caged possessively around my lower half.

I shiver as he runs a claw down the cleft of my ass, half a moan escaping me at the sensation of his probing against the last twitching aftershocks of my orgasm. He gives a low, rumbly chuckle in response, and I can feel the vibrations of it through my chest against his.

"Why do you wear that cloak anyway?" I murmur, tracing patterns through the suede-like feel of his fuzz.

"It's slimming," he hums.

"Oh," I nod, and bite down against a smile. I suppose it is easier to fit through doorways when you have less of a physical form. I can't imagine him getting on the lift when he's this size. Perhaps it's also better for avoiding getting stabbed. It's strange to think of the office outside this Dark Sanctum, the messages and the stacks of paperwork. All of it seems so mundane compared to the rituals Soven performs in here.

I'll have to leave him to it, in a little bit, I realize. I have to get dressed and go back out there, and resume my work day. I may have offered up my body to his dark bidding, but that's not very different from giving him my time and effort, day in and day out.

A quiet lull falls over us. Even as I lay my head on his massive chest, all I can hear is his breath.

"How come I can't feel a heartbeat?" I ask, tracing circles in the fuzz of his flesh.

"I don't have a heart. I have a reliquary," he says simply.

I wrinkle my nose, unsure if I want to know. "A what?"

Soven hesitates, and I wonder if I've asked something I shouldn't have.

"It's just a type of container," he shrugs after a moment. "With blood and bones in it. As well as the entirety of my power. Most Liches hide their reliquaries miles away, at the bottom of impossible dungeons. That way, anyone who attacks you in person cannot kill you."

He explains it to me in that teacher sort of voice. Sometimes when he does that, I think it's such a shame he doesn't have an apprentice. I think it would make him so happy.

"But if they got to the bottom of the dungeon where it's hidden, they could," I worry.

"Like I said," he chuckles. "You want to keep it safe."

I nodded against him, my hand digging into his chest a little. To me, it sounds like this reliquary thing is basically his heart. I can't imagine burying my heart or liver or kidneys or anything vital underground in a box.

But he's buried his heart in some rotten dungeon somewhere, where no one can ever get to it. The thought sort of saddens me.

Insecurity creeps in alongside that thought. He's the Dark Lord—I can't have been the first to have stripped in front of him and told him to fuck me into Wednesday.

"Well, um, I should get back to work," I say, sitting up and looking around for my clothes.

I am still just his secretary, after all.

5

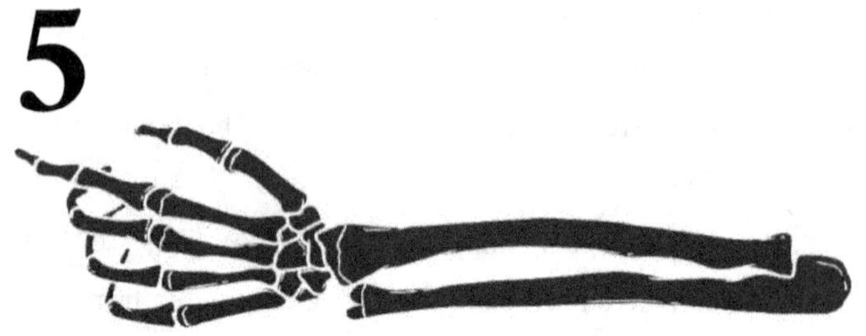

"I just don't think it's a healthy workplace dynamic," Janice from HR says during lunch. We've gotten a cafeteria table across from one another.

"I mean, giving away shivers? What if next he needs a quart of sweat, or to pluck all of your left eyelashes out? There's so much paperwork involved, and the union to work with," she continues on, waving around a forkful of her salad, losing some of her vinaigrette in the process.

"It was only a shiver," I shrug, as if it was a one-time thing that I hadn't drastically escalated since. "Besides, I'm not part of a union."

"Well, then that's another side of the problem, isn't it?" Janice rolls her eyes as she chews through a mouthful. "I mean, gods, that's why the downstairs security is so heavy. The number of weirdos that used to come in and prostrate themselves before their Dark Lord; it happened at least once a week when the Lich Lord first took over. It was slowing things down, that's why we had to outsource through other agencies."

I didn't know that. Somehow not knowing makes me feel extraordinarily stupid and naïve. I fumble to keep my composure while something like jealousy and despair rises in my throat, and fights to be let out. I swallow a few times, holding my mouth in a firm line.

"And now we have to screen for assassins who've infiltrated the agencies and unions and whatever," I scoff, but a little too much emotion comes out in the words. I need to reel it in or she's bound to wonder why I care so much about 'just a shiver'.

But Janice doesn't seem to notice, taking my derision as annoyance at having my desk obliterated because of said assassins.

It's been weighing more and more on me these last few days since I was the weirdo to prostrate myself before my Dark Lord and offer up my body to him.

The thought of offering my heart to him as well won't leave my mind, no matter how I try to shunt it to the side or bury it under a pile of lust, as if that will make those feelings dissolve into mere lust as well.

I want him to know, but more than that I want him to return those feelings. But if I confess my feelings to him, and he either can't or won't return them, I don't know if I'll be able to continue working here. It might be too awkward to bear, or too painful to continue seeing him every day.

And I really like working here. It's not just the health benefits. I feel needed and important. I don't know that anywhere else will give me that kind of satisfaction. I guess that's kind of one of the pitfalls of working in an evil dominion; there really isn't anywhere else to work.

Still, the thought preoccupies me almost all day. Every time I have to dip into Soven's Sanctum, something in my heart pinches when I look at him, and I feel like I need to duck out of the Sanctum again to avoid that feeling.

I step into the Sanctum, walking quickly to his desk to deposit a stack of internal reports. I turn on a dime the moment I put the folders down. I don't really want to give him the time to hold a conversation, or say anything not work related.

"Lily, do you--" he starts to ask, but when I glance back, my expression stops him.

I can feel the mix of panic and discomfort showing plain on my face.

"Is it urgent?" I ask, giving him my best 'I'm way too busy right now' look. I feel like if I tried to explain the way all my feelings are swirling together in my stomach like an ill-conceived smoothie, I would just spill my guts, figuratively, literally, or both.

Soven shakes his head and returns his gaze to his desk. "Never mind."

What if I've read too much into this, thinking that because we've developed an ease with each other, that that's the same as romantic feelings? What if I clearly think too much of myself, that a human could ever mean anything to an all-powerful Lich?

By the time I finally push my worries down enough with my work, it's after hours. I don't want to think about how much time I must have spent dithering over my feelings.

I quickly finish up the seating chart for the next office-wide meeting that I was working on, the last person in the office. The desks are all empty and quiet. It's as good a time as any to move my things back to the waiting room.

The recently obliterated waiting room has been spackled, painted and refurnished, so I'm moving my things preemptively to my brand new desk, raiding the cabinet for all the paperclips and quills I can carry.

The office is so quiet and empty, I'm surprised to see Soven standing by the water cooler on my third trip back and forth. I'm a little startled, because he's still out of his cloak, and I've never seen him in the office without it.

I give him a skeptical look, glancing around at the empty cubicles, the darkened windows, but I cross over to where he stands. I do bite down on a 'How did you fit through the doorway?'

"What's going on?"

"I've always wanted to do this," he says, and I blink at him in confusion.

"What do you mean?"

Soven gives himself a little shake, shrugging. I can see how he's only pretending to lean against the water cooler, that way none of his weight actually presses down on it. He plucks two of the little paper cups out from the dispenser, handing one to me. I fill mine with cold water.

Then Soven says, "Workin' hard, or hardly workin'?"

He snaps and points a claw out over the empty cubicle, and pretends to wink at some imaginary coworker. It's so overwhelmingly ridiculous to imagine him working in one of these tiny cubicles, I can't help but laugh.

"You're such a dork," I say, putting a hand over my mouth. "No one actually says that."

"Would it help productivity if I put out a memo to have it integrated into the common parlance? Alongside 'synergy' and 'incentivize'?"

I laugh-cough into my paper cup.

"Stop, stop," I say, holding up my hands in surrender. "You're gonna get water up my nose!"

Laughter dies down between us, the ache of smiling imprinted in my cheeks as I sigh and stifle a leftover giggle. Then it's quiet for a long moment, and suddenly I don't want this little moment between us to end. It's different from when we're in the dark sanctum, bodies slick with sweat and cum and still rutting against each other for just one more release. Somehow I'd thought that we wouldn't have these fun little moments anymore. It's quiet and soft, and suddenly my whole chest is brimming with the feelings I want to tell him.

I cough, and clear my throat, taking a different tact. "So… whatever made you start the whole, evil empire thing?"

"It wasn't exactly a plan of mine," he shrugs. "Being a Lich is... characterized by unending greed. To live, to constantly take in day after day of life, all that comes with them, and never being willing to relinquish any of it. It becomes a lonely, hoarding existence."

"So you just collect things forever? I mean, is there anything you've had to give up?" I ask, the question clunky even as I say it. I might as well ask, 'Is it even possible for you to love me back?'

He shrugs a little, and while I can see the question almost turn over in his mind, he seems to get lost in his thoughts. I guess it was that hard of a question.

We lapse into a long silence again, and I have to wonder if he could feel the question hovering on my lips, even unasked.

"Well, um, I have something for you," he says, clearing his throat, straightening as he faces me. I look at him in surprise, and feel a faint flutter of excitement over my organs, I think my liver. Briefly I remember the flowers he had left on my desk. I don't think I realized how much I wanted some small romantic gesture from Soven, unfettered, unabashed, until this moment. Something that clearly demonstrated feelings or intent.

I can see him holding back a smile, or as close to a smile as he can have with the structure of his fangs. "You've been here with us for a while now, so I'd like to present to you, your five-year-gift," he says, producing a somewhat generic looking necklace, a pendant with the Evil Reign's insignia stamped on one side, and a red stone on the other side.

I blink, frozen.

Soven takes this as a good moment to fit the necklace over my head.

"I thought I was supposed to pick something from the company catalog for that," I stammer out, the only thought in my head that isn't crashing disappointment. I barely want to admit to myself what I'm disappointed about, what I'd been getting my hopes up for. Something heartfelt. Something like those flowers, without the card that made them feel less like a romantic gesture and more like an apology.

"That's for the ten year gift," he shrugs. He looks so pleased with himself, having given me this congratulatory anniversary gift.

Then he seems to take in my less-than-enthused reaction. "You... don't like it?"

"It's lovely," I say quickly. "I'll, um, treasure it always."

He gives me another sort of grin around his fangs, and my heart sinks a little. I can't keep getting my hopes up with him.

6

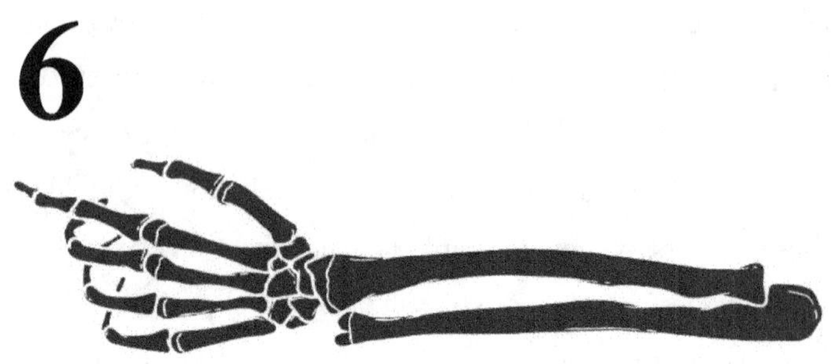

When I came in to work the next day, my desk was decorated with confetti. My old, cleaned out cubicle, that is.

The rest of the office apparently knew it was my five-year anniversary, and Janice had even taken the opportunity to bring in sugarless cupcakes. I honestly still can't tell if that was a kind gesture or not.

At least they didn't know I'd already moved desks, and my actual working desk in the Dark Sanctum's waiting room is still perfectly clean. Still, I linger out at the emptied cubicle with my planner, figuring out my day's to-do list while accepting various good wishes from the accounting department. Randall even gives me a card, which is unexpectedly sweet of him.

I duck into the washroom after someone releases a handful of confetti over my head alongside their happy-five-years proclamations and as I'm picking the pieces out of my hair, my eyes fall on the necklace chain that leads under my dress, the pendant hidden under my collar.

I'd spent every spare moment I had before work trying to decide whether or not to wear it at all. It was a little cheesy, wearing a necklace with the Evil Regime's symbol on it to the office. It's not like I need to advertise to everyone.

But Soven had looked so proud of himself after giving it to me, I felt guilty leaving it at home. It wasn't that it wasn't lovely; it was what it meant. Or all the things it didn't mean that I had hoped it would, like some silly, stupid mortal would. Eventually I had compromised and worn it, but tucked it under my top.

I fidget with the chain a moment, before eventually deciding to pull it out, and let it sit on display over my breast. If there would be one day to wear it, I guess it would have to be my five-year anniversary at this job.

I wear it out to the office, returning to my desk in the waiting room.

It's oddly quiet here, and I don't know if I like that. I've been craving this quiet, this privacy, all week while waiting to have my desk back, but now I don't have anything to distract me from eyeing the small space between my desk and the doors of the Dark Sanctum.

It's as I glance the other direction, that it hits me. The ceiling to floor long window is gone. I used to be able to look out of it across the office, wave at people sitting in the cubicles. Now there's just a wall there.

It's isolating. Why on earth would Soven get rid of the window?

I jump as I hear Soven call my name from the other side of those doors.

"Lily?"

I sit still and stare for a moment. Of course he'd know I'd be here, this is where I usually am. I don't know if I'm dreading or hoping to cross that threshold between us. I know I can't stop thinking about him, but I also know how easily he could break my heart.

I stand, and take a moment to smooth out my skirt, like it will make any difference. He's seen me beyond disheveled before. I'm delaying.

I open the Sanctum doors, peering inside. As my eyes adjust to the light, I see that his desk is empty. My brows furrow, as my gaze drifts over the built in bookshelves and cases of ingredients, and the small library of alchemical texts.

"You called, Soven?" I call out, looking around in all the usual spots. While it's still at the forefront of my mind, I ask, "And what's with the uh, whole thing about my window being gone?"

Then I spot Soven, in the middle of the ritual floor.

The altar is different than usual. Today it's a seat large enough to accommodate Soven, and he leans back comfortably in it, naked, three dicks draped artfully over his thigh.

I am a little flustered to see him like this, after all, it is first thing in the morning.

The sight of him, the knowledge of the passion and exhilaration that he can provoke in my body during these rituals, instantly ignites a warmth low in my stomach and kindles a wetness between my legs.

"Oh," I say, shutting the door behind me and crossing to stand before him. I feel a little silly, having brought in my planner and itinerary for the day, as well as a freshly inked quill. I doubt very much he wants to hear if he has any messages or appointments right now.

Soven nods, gesturing me to come closer with his claw. I quickly abandon my planner and quill to the nearest table, step up onto the platform, sidling into his lap, as has become somewhat normal for us in the last week.

"I have something new for you today," he purrs, tracing his claw down the cleft of my cheeks through my skirt.

My body responds with a wave of heat and a flutter of excitement. "What is it?"

He opens a glass bottle full of a dark blue liquid that shimmers in the candlelight. I watch as he reaches over to a table, picking up something small.

Soven catches my eye, the curiosity plain on my face. "Lift your skirt," he nods to me.

I lean back in his lap, pulling my skirt up to my stomach, spreading my legs wide.

"This is the surprise?" I ask, my eyes on the little thing in his hand. It's metallic, sort of egg shaped, until it flares out at the bottom. It takes me a moment before I realize where I've seen one of those before. *Oh.*

"This is for preparation," he says, dipping it in the bottle of shimmery liquid.

"You have… another ritual in mind?" I ask, glancing around where we stand. The runes are dim, the candles burn a normal color.

Soven holds my gaze and after a moment, nods. "One I think you'll enjoy."

My faces heats up as I think about it. I'm excited by the idea of him exploring me fully, pushing me to my limits, but something snags in my mind. What if I'm getting too tangled up in him and these rituals and my feelings?

I must get a little too lost in my thoughts, because he pulls me from them, brushing my hair back from my face with a gentle stroke of his claw.

"Ready?" he rumbles, grazing that precise, careful touch down my cheek.

I could say no, and push away from him. Push away from all these feelings clouding my heart, distracting me from my job. It's not in me to break my own heart though. I don't think I could give up all these moments with him just to protect my heart.

I nod, and he turns me over to lay on my back, dragging his long, hot tongue through the cleft of my ass cheeks. The feeling almost like when he fucked me from behind on his largest dick, the way the little sucker on his top cock would graze and tease my asshole. After a few licks, I can feel him press the toy at my entrance.

"Do it," I say, firmer in my resolve. I meant it that first day that I wanted him to need me.

He pushes the toy a little harder, I gasp aloud as it penetrates my ass, slick and easy, sliding inside me and staying there. The pressure of it is new and I want more of it.

And then, that's it.

I wait for more for a few seconds, wondering if he's giving me a moment to adjust. A few too many moments go by with no new sensations, no new experimentation. I sit up and look at Soven.

"That will be all," he says, bottling the liquid up again.

I frown, perplexed. That's really it?

When it appears that is indeed everything, I hop off his lap and brush down my skirt into place. I'll have his little toy in me all day long, and the thought of that secret between us makes me smile.

I start to cross the Sanctum back to my desk, when the toy gives a little pulse of pleasure, stopping me in my tracks.

I stop and look back at Soven, the lazy way he strokes a large hand up and down his third, bottom cock. That one has yet to be in me, or really take part in our activities. I'd been beginning to wonder if it had any use at all.

My face lights up as I put the pieces together, and Soven chuckles at my eagerness.

I slip outside the Dark Sanctum, leaving the door open a sliver. When I sit down at my desk, I can still smell the freshness of the paint from time to time, but that's hardly at the forefront of my mind as I sit down and feel the way the toy stretches my hole, the press of it inside me.

Preparation, right.

7

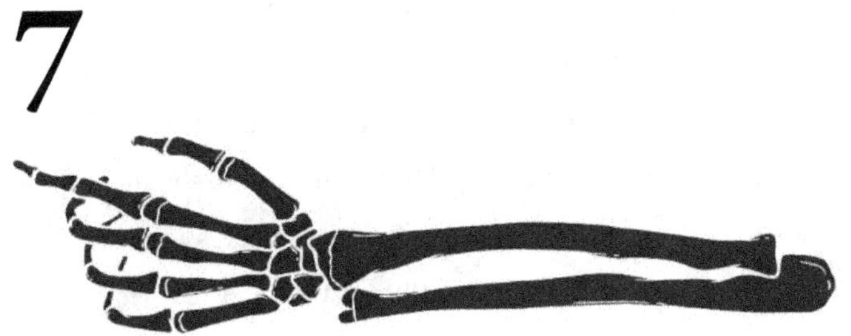

Every so often I look up from my work, when Soven pauses and catches my eye through the Dark Sanctum door, and a thrill of excitement runs through me. Our secret.

I brace myself, knowing his magic will flex and stretch the toy, furthering my limits. Each time it does, the pulse makes me shiver and aroused all over again. I wish it would last longer. Each little taste of pleasure is far too short for my taste. A number of times I think about locking the waiting room door and rubbing one out, just to finish off what his toy keeps teasing me with. I think I might die from being fucked too slowly. The only thing that keeps me in my seat, patiently taking the torturous pulses of the toy is the thought of finally being thoroughly fucked on all three of Soven's cocks.

I still when I glance at the clock, realizing that in all likelihood I'll have to go to the office-wide meeting with it still in me. I know Soven wouldn't want to skip the meeting, since he's the one conducting it. The idea makes me warm all over, and I press my knees together hard under my desk.

I leave my desk to set up the presentation materials for the meeting. Maybe half an hour in, I realize I haven't felt the toy move at all. It really only pulses when I look Soven in the eyes, I suppose. Without its teasing, it's become so comfortable in me that I don't even really notice it's there.

I'm in the meeting room arranging extra chairs when Soven enters the door.

There's something almost weird about seeing him in the cloak again, the way the cloak's hood has no expression, the way he floats ominously a few feet away from me, a benign spectre of death. I guess I've become too used to seeing his true body, and being pressed up against it.

"Where are this last month's growth charts?" he asks. It's his voice, but the disembodied way it comes from him is jarring.

"Here they are," I say, pulling out one of the folders from under a stack. I present the folder to Soven, and he takes it, opening it to scan the contents while I stand beside him.

I realize I'm waiting like some kind of trained pet, waiting for him to pulse the toy again, or touch my cheek, or some kind of acknowledgement.

This shouldn't feel as… alienating as it does. We're doing our jobs. I'm doing all the personal assistant things I've always done.

"Can we compare these numbers with those of this month last year?" he asks, and I nod quickly.

"I can fetch those from the records room," I nod, my gaze falling to the floor. I feel like it stands out how ridiculous I'm being, waiting for a caress that will never come.

The distant, cold feeling stays with me as I leave, and go into the records room. Throughout this week I've passed by this room a number of times and it started to snag my interest, when a horrible thought entered my head. The kind of curious thought that will lead nowhere but pain, but once the question has been asked, it haunts your mind.

I find the records of business with outside agencies, and stop in front of the filing cabinet. I know it's wrong. It's practically stalking. It isn't my business to know how many agencies we contracted out to for sex rituals, if any.

I don't even know what the answer is going to tell me, if I look. So what if he has brought other humans into his ritual space for sex magic? Who am I to slutshame my Dark Lord?

But at the same time, the cold worry that clings to my spine hints that perhaps if there are a decent amount of records of people who have taken part in these rituals, it will imply that I'm just another body filling a space, producing the sensations he needs as ingredients. I'm just another item on the inventory spreadsheet.

I pull the drawer open a few inches, but as I start to look over the folders organized within, I slam it shut again. I don't think I want to know. I'm not ready to ask that question.

Maybe I'm getting too lost in my own head. I need to get back to the meeting.

I cross the room to another file cabinet, and pull open the drawer for last years' numbers. I pull the file out quickly, and as I'm shutting the drawer, a glint in the light catches my eye on one of the shelves.

It's one of the storage shelves filled with backup ingredients for Soven's rituals. Most of it is inert, shelf-stable stuff: powders and dried herbs, minerals and whatnot. It's next to the paper supplies shelves that people take too many paperclips from. Usually when I need to take inventory, I run through this shelf first.

There's a soft purple vial though, that seems to shimmer in the light. It sticks out of place, and I'm sure I've never seen it here before. I touch it as delicately as I can, turning it around to view the label.

'Lily, Shiver', it reads, with the date I let Soven caress my skin on the vial. Staring at the label, my eyes start to tear up.

He never even used the shiver he got from me. He just… put it in the storage room.

I don't know how I got it into my head that we were more than boss and employee, Evil Overlord and subjugated servant. He never asked for my heart, I don't know why I thought I should throw it in with offering up my body.

I will not cry at work. I won't. Even as my chest tightens, I wave a hand at my eyes, willing the tears back so they won't disturb my makeup. I breathe in and out too fast, swallowing until I've pushed the crying feeling back down my throat.

I exit the records room quickly, hoping the walk will help clear the thickness in my throat and the way my nose feels like it's already starting to drip.

The meeting's already started. I must have taken too long in the records room. I'm walking quickly through the rows of empty cubicles when I see Randall in my path, waving me down.

"Lily! I thought you'd be at the office-wide meeting," he says. He doesn't say anything about mascara streaks on my face, so I assume I managed to hold in my tears well enough not to make a mess of myself.

I give a weak shrug. "Oh. Yeah, well. I needed to run and grab a file for it. What about you?"

"I just stepped out for a moment."

I nod and begin to move past him, when he clears his throat and says quickly, "Would you, erm, well, uh, ever think about getting coffee?"

I blink a couple times, my head still in such a fog of emotions from the record room, that his question seems absurdly mundane. It's like asking if I can restock the paperclips.

"What?"

"I mean, that is," he coughs, tugging at his collar. "With me?"

Oh. I stare at Randall for a long moment as I realize his meaning. Wow, what a bad moment to ask. I glance around the empty office. Maybe because we're alone, and he can't see the aura of disappointment and self-pity haunting my head, it seems like a good time to him.

"Sure," I shrug, because why the fuck not. Maybe I've never really found anything particularly romantic about Randall, but he's nice.

Coffee with him is harmless. It's not recklessly throwing my heart to someone who won't take it. At worst, I'll probably dump my feelings from the past week on him and cry my heart out to a sort of friend, maybe at best I'll find a kernel of the affection I've been so starved for.

"Alright, it's a date," he says, giving me a sweet smile.

And then the room starts to rumble. Cracks form in the floor, dark clouds begin to swirl.

I jump back from a crack in the ground, where a pit is opening up. I can see the HR department on the floor beneath us, the cracks forming there too. I look up and my eyes fall on the only one who could be doing this.

Soven gestures to Randall, who falls into the pit, pushed by some invisible force. He and the sound of his yells quickly disappear as he plummets through the building's floors faster than the elevator could take him.

The ground seals back up again, clearly damaged but walkable, as Soven passes over it and heads towards his office, meeting apparently canceled.

Coffee with Randall is not so harmless, it seems.

8

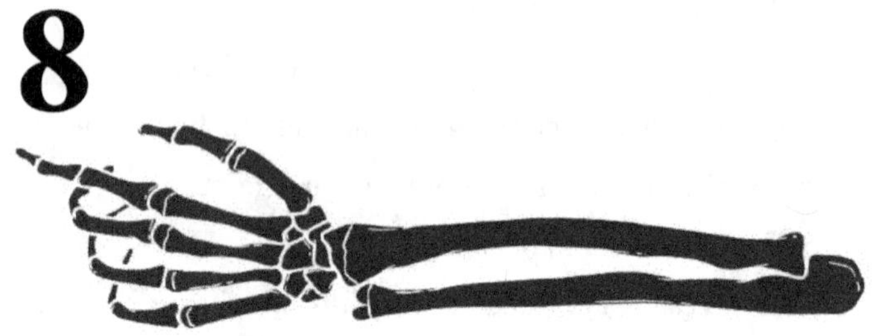

This is the last straw. I'm spitting mad, but at the same time, it's tearing me apart inside thinking that this is the last straw. I am standing at the edge of a precipice here, metaphorical, literal or whatever.

I march into Soven's office and all but shove the heavy doors behind me closed. They pivot slowly on their hinges and don't slam quite as much as I want for dramatic effect. I bristle and cross my arms at the Lich in front of me.

"*What the hell was that about?*" I snap at Soven. I've never raised my voice so angrily at him before, and yet this does not seem to shock him.

"Downsizing," Soven growls, throwing off his cloak of shadows, revealing the beast underneath.

I gawk for a moment, and all I can seem to gather up to return is, "It's wrongful dismissal, and you know it!"

Soven avoids looking at me as he stalks around the darkened Sanctum. He makes a noise like a wrongful dismissal suit isn't a problem. And under the Evil Regime, it probably isn't.

But that's not the point. Or maybe it is. All I know is all my barely contained emotions break through to the surface, and suddenly it's about us.

"No, you can't do this to me!"

"Do what," he growls, less of a question and more bait.

"This, all of this, you can't disregard my personal agency and throw Randall down a pit! It's insane and I don't want any of it!" I snap, looking wildly at Soven, stomping my way over to him.

He draws himself up to his full, ridiculous height at my, quite frankly, comparatively tiny fit. Soven holds me in his gaze for many long moments, during all of which I'm fuming.

"You enjoyed the flowers, I assume?" he says at last, thumbing the fur at the end of his jowls.

I nearly roll my eyes. "That's beside the point, everyone likes flowers—"

"But not the intern," he interrupts, "Who you refuse to delegate assignments to."

"No—"

"And you accepted the five-year-gift."

"I did, but—"

"But not the office. Even though you've wanted a real office of your own for years," he says, like this is some kind of gift. I'm surprised he knew, but that doesn't get him out of trouble for going ahead and changing things around without my knowledge. He could have at least asked!

"You can't – push the intern onto me, or move my desk where I can't see people, or banish someone for asking me out!" I nearly shout in response, because clearly he isn't getting it. I don't know what the norms are for hooking up with a Lich, but I did not sign up for unprovoked territorialism.

"If I cannot share my pleasures, my power, and my privileges with you—" Soven starts, and I cut him off instantly.

I pull out the chair from his desk, and stand up on it to look him in the eye.

"But it's not sharing, is it? If it's pushed upon me without consultation, then what am I but another piece in the hoard you control? How am I supposed to be ok with us, when there isn't any respect between us? I barely even feel like there is an 'us'!"

I see the flame spark in his eye at that, and clearly I've touched a nerve. I watch him struggle internally for what to do with his hands, his claws flexing dangerously at his side before he paces away, tearing them through his mane.

"Respect? How can you bring up respect when you accept his advances? How can you—" he looks away from me, struggling for the words he wants. "—After all I've shown you?"

Shown me? What?

I stare at him, indignation and upset bubbling up among some new heartbreak as I realize his meaning, the implication of his feelings.

No, he doesn't get to make this my fault. Not when this is the first time he's even broached the idea that he can have feelings for me.

"You've shown me nothing, no hint about what you're feeling. For all I know, I'm only skin and sensations for you to take from. And you—you put my shiver in the storage closet, you didn't even use it!" I say, and those are the words that finally exhaust my anger. That there could have been feelings between us this whole time, and I'd been locked out of them, that I'd been made to feel like I was just another piece of office supplies to him. "I gave my body to you, and I would have given you my heart too, if I thought you wanted it. But I can't give it if it's just going to be part of your hoard," I say, and that's all I can get out as my voice wavers dangerously. Ok, I might cry at work. But I won't cry in front of my boss.

I can't look at Soven after that. I turn on my heel and leave.

9

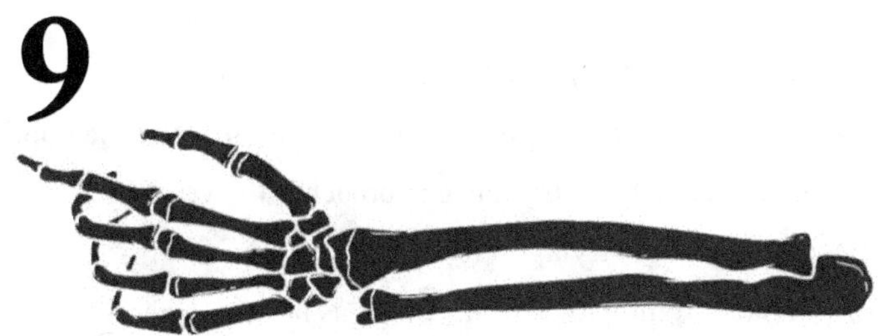

Janice looks up from her desk as I approach, her expression becoming confused as she takes in my significantly more lifeless than usual state.

"I think I might be getting fired soon," I sigh, too exhausted to give any emotional weight to the statement. I think if I tried, I'd crack open and blubber about it for hours.

"What? What's going on?" she asks, looking a bit alarmed. I don't usually visit her during the workday.

"C'mon, smoke break."

"We don't even smoke—"

"Then we'll start, or whatever. Coffee, we'll get coffee," I grumble, pulling her up from her desk in an attempt to drag her along with me. She gets up and pulls out of my grip, but follows me out to one of the break rooms on a lower floor. "Although, apparently that's a fireable offense now."

I wait until we get to one of the break rooms, and the door swings closed behind us. Janice approaches the vending machine and starts trying to feed it coins.

"I had a fight with Soven," I sigh as her coins plunk through the slot, one by one. "I stood on a table and yelled at him."

"…Yeah, I think there's no coming back from that," she concedes after a moment. She doesn't ask if it was before or after the pit opening up in the office floor.

I nod weakly. I don't know how to explain all of it, why I had to stand on a desk.

"It wasn't just a shiver," I say at last.

"I had a feeling," she says, rolling her eyes. Sounds like she hadn't really believed me when I'd told her about the shiver initially.

I give her a rundown of the last few days, not sparing any detail except about Soven's absurd number of cocks, though I wondered if it might make her any more sympathetic to my motives.

"Are you sure you didn't get a promotion from secretary to sex slave?" she asks, looking somewhat unimpressed with me.

"I'd think there'd be a change in my benefits programs," I say dryly.

"I mean, new desk, an intern to delegate to, those are the perks of dating your boss," she shrugs. "Alongside getting taken advantage of, nepotism, lack of boundaries—"

"Hang on. I'm the one who seduced him; he's not taking advantage of me."

"What are you saying? You want to file a harassment claim against yourself?" She rolls her eyes and gives me a look. "Honey. He's the one with the power to fire you."

I hang my head and sigh, because I hadn't thought about how badly things could go. When I had first kissed Soven, all I could think about was how exhilarating it was, how his body made mine react. All our goofy chats in the office had only ever brought us closer and closer, of course I never thought this would drive us apart, and be unable to ever have that again.

I let Janice go back to her desk, despite her offers to try to handle whatever comes next with me.

I go into the waiting room, my office, whatever it is, with a cardboard box.

As soon as I push through the door, however, I can see Soven waiting for me, his full beast form hunched over my desk, crowded into one of the waiting room chairs.

I approach slowly, wondering if I should ask him if he wants me to tender my resignation. He hadn't yet banished me through a hole in the floor though, so maybe it'll be more like a two-week notice while I find someone to replace me.

He looks up as I cross the room, unfurling himself from the ways he's knotted his limbs together to fit into the human-sized chair.

Slowly he rises, his stare held carefully upon me.

I swallow and look to the floor awkwardly, running my thumbs along the cardboard box while I try to kick my brain into thinking. I don't know how to start this conversation.

I don't have to, apparently, when he brings one curled fist before him. His claws fall open, to show he had two vials curled up in his hand, one I recognize by its soft lilac glow. My shiver.

"I couldn't bring myself to waste one bit of you," he murmurs, and those words make my heart ache.

My eyes are filling up with tears. I've been such an idiot. He's been so careful, so precise with me, how could I ever think that was anything but his way of expressing tenderness?

"I cannot give you my heart," he says, voice low and guttural. He brings out his other massive hand, to pluck up the second vial from his palm and hold it out to me. "As I have none."

I study the vial in front of my eyes, the inky darkness in its deep red contents, the way it seems to pull shadows into it.

"This is—"

"My reliquary," he nods slowly, holding it out. "If you take it, I hope you will be protective of it. But I will ask first if you want it."

I have no words. My throat is so tight with emotion I can barely nod. I bring a shaking hand up to take the reliquary from him. The glass is cool to touch, and just holding it, I sense it's more fragile than a heart.

"I'll keep it somewhere safe," I promise, looking up at him as the tears spill down over my cheeks. I sniffle as he brushes them away with the back of his knuckle.

He makes a gesture, and the vial of my shiver disappears into mist, likely tucked away somewhere only he can reach.

I tilt my head back for him, and he drags a kiss along my jaw, brushing his cheek against mine, the suede of his body gently grazing my skin. I give a soft gasp as I feel the toy pulse again deliciously, a flirtatious touch of his magic, so comfortable in my ass I'd all but forgotten its presence there.

I look up at Soven, unable to disguise my excitement. His claws graze carefully down my body, as he crowds me backwards, coaxing me to sit on my desk.

He drags a claw through his teeth, sharpening the edge before he draws it up my pencil skirt, my blouse, the sound of fabric slicing open, falling off and around me, petal soft.

It's as I lean back on the table, spreading my legs apart, that I realize this isn't for a ritual. There's no alchemical circle drawn, no runes, no candles. This is purely for us.

The thought makes me pause, as more warm tears well up in my eyes. As much as his magic intrigued me, this is what I've really wanted: just a girl and her undying Lich lover.

I think Soven realizes it too, because he does something he hadn't done before in our previous sex magic rituals-- he kisses my forehead, carefully combing his claws through my hair. He takes a long moment to just trace my neck, my arms, my waist and thighs appreciatively, his gaze lingering, marveling at all the new territory we have to be soft with one another.

The toy gives another few pulses, warming my body up as Soven parts my ass cheeks, slowly teasing the toy out. The sheer tenderness of it serves as a prelude for how thoroughly he will fuck me on all of his cocks.

His fingers trail up my stomach from where he held my hip, to graze against my breast. He looks at my face again, and I nod, quivering with anticipation, aching at how slowly he moves over me, and relishing in it.

He places a hand over my breast, working his way to my nipples, thumb rolling over them, hard and perky, and listens hard to my little gasps, the way my hips twitch and stutter helplessly as I melt under his touch.

"Let me know if I should stop," he murmurs, in a voice soft and deep, looking into my eyes. I bite my lip and nod again. He presses a kiss to my forehead, and begins to work his way down.

I don't know why he would think I would ever ask him to stop.

Even though we've done this all before, it's different. In some strange way, it feels like our first time all over again, in the way each movement holds reverence in its exploration. There's some new excitement in knowing that everything he does is because he wants to, not because it's part of a ritual.

He licks my tits, sucking on them, grazing his teeth against them, unraveling my composure with the utmost precision and care. Soon I can't contain the noises of pleasure, moans and keens of 'keep doing that please'.

As he continues to kiss and caress my breast, he trails a clawed hand down my stomach, a shiver going through my belly.

My hands drift down his tight abdomen, finding his cocks hot and hard, ready to take me. His second cock is thick and heavy in my hand, too much for me to properly hold. Even as I stroke him up and down, for a moment it makes me doubt whether or not it would go inside me properly without being fucked open on his tongue again.

His enjoyment is clear, however, the way pre-cum beads at the tip of his cocks. He tilts his head back, letting out a sound half sigh, half moan. "Lily… if only you knew the power you have over me."

I lick my lips and bite down against my smile. "Well. I'll keep that in mind next time I want to ask for a raise."

He chuckles, the sound going right to my thighs.

After a moment, he gestures for me to lay down. He hunches over me and kisses my breast again, I can feel his engorged cocks pressed hard against my stomach as he pulls me close, parting my knees, positioning me.

"Before, when you said, 'use me'…" Soven starts to say, the trails off.

"What about it?"

He shakes his head a little. "I don't know that I could fulfill that request properly. You're not just an ingredient in a spell."

As he says this, his cocks graze up against my entrances, drawing his middle cock wet and leaking up my center to part my cunt's lips. Roving hands feel me thoroughly, searching until he finds my cunt soaked and wanting, poised himself and pushed in.

I try not to moan at how he feels inside me, how nicely he fits after I had been aching for him to fill me, stretch me to my limits. At first the one was more than enough to make my hips twitch as he worked in and out of my cunt, but then the press of his third cock against my hole made me realize how much more I wanted.

I catch my breath, looking up at him. I reach up and touch his face. He leans into my palm. "I know."

"You're not a means to an end. You are the end."

I think my heart is so full it might burst. "You're my end too."

He grins, as much as his beastly face will allow. His half lidded eyes dip down across me, taking me in, and I watch him taste my wetness off his claws. I whimper. I have a thousand things to say, all of them yes and please, do whatever you want with me.

I watch, near breathless and quivering as he slathers the lubricant along his third cock, the bottle plucked from thin air. I hope he has several more stowed away somewhere for the days we'll have ahead of us.

I tense as he eases the very tip of his third cock in my ass.

He thrusts once, and everything slides into place, his top cock connecting with my clit, a spark of sensation against the fullness of his cocks entirely inside me. My hands curl around his horns, as I shift my hips experimentally, feeling every doubly penetrating inch slide in and out of me.

Soon enough he's pounding into me, every nerve in my body on fire, stripped and raw and sparking with sensation. I lose count after the second orgasm, I lose track of time, and I lose the ability to make any noise but a moan or a scream.

It doesn't matter, as long as I have Soven.

My hand curls tight around his reliquary and I hold it to my chest.

Janice

As an HR professional, I cannot just stand by during all this.

As Lily's friend, I don't know what to say.

I mean, work friends. It's not like we're sorority sisters or anything. Maybe that's it. Maybe that's where the line is. Maybe all of it is truly none of my business, and filing a report about our CEO is out of my area of influence.

"No, I cannot. I cannot hear what our boss's dick looks like, that's just– that's out of my pay grade," I tell her, interrupting the elaborate miming she's doing across the table from me in the break room.

"DICKS," she repeats with terrible emphasis, and hand gestures.

"LILY," I plead, "I can't hear any of this."

Because if she keeps telling me all the things she should not be doing, I'm going to have to say something. I don't know why I haven't done something about it already.

Then again, considering what happened to Randall, maybe I'm not going to say anything about it. Soven might snap his fingers and the floor would swallow me up. And our company's severance package is just terrible.

Normally at work, watching coworkers make poor life decisions is none of my business. Normally it falls outside the bounds of my job. I just repeat what they say back to me.

Oh, you're getting into NFTs? Wow, good for you I guess. No, I don't want to join your #girlboss pyramid scheme, thanks. No, I don't care that you swear by the products. Oh, you're not contributing to your 401K? Actually, let's schedule a meeting to go over how that works, because that actually is my job. Our company matches up to 6% of your contributions, so you should really rethink that.

Minding your own business is an art form. The veneer is coming off the art, though.

"Just," I pinch the bridge of my nose. She looks so incandescently happy, I don't have it in me to rain on her parade. "Just document everything. That's all I'm going to say."

She chews through a bite of her food. She looks from left to right, like she's missing something. "What am I doing, right now?"

I know a lot of people treat her like she's just the dumb, cute secretary. I know from talking to her that that just isn't true: she's plenty capable. She is downright terrifying with spreadsheets. But sometimes this girl really makes me wonder.

"There has got to be a line between documentation and describing the CEO's dicks in detail," I deadpan.

"You don't understand, it was magical," she goes on, like nothing I'm saying is registering. Of course it isn't, she's all caught up in her feelings and rosy colored glasses.

"Oh, there was magic involved. I don't think that makes it better, I think there's a good chance that makes it even worse," I tell her.

She's younger than me by enough that I guess I can understand why the whole 'hooking up with your boss' sounds exciting and not just one red flag after another.

The stare I give Lily is long, hard, and heavily judgmental. "You don't think dating your boss is a little problematic?"

She sighs, blowing some of her bangs out of her face. "Not as much as I think our company's PTO policy is."

I sigh and rub my temples, trying not to smear my eyebrow pencil. Arguing with her right now is getting me exactly nowhere. Fine, I'll let things cool off a bit. But then I'm coming right back to this topic.

Office relationships are a mistake, and there isn't anything that can convince me otherwise.

1

THE ORC FROM THE OFFICE (Claws & Cubicles 2)

What irresponsible, fucking— ugh! Who the hell shuts a drawer this tight?!

I let out a small noise of frustration, rattling the entire metal filing cabinet as I wrestle with the one drawer that I need to stick this report in. That noise is the only hint that I'm losing my cool, and to a piece of furniture, no less.

You would think that working at a company chaired by a board of undead and a spearheaded by a fearsome necromancer, this kind of petty thing would be expected. On the contrary. I expect my coworkers at Evil Inc. to have some standards for how they file things away.

I step back, dusting off my shirt even though it's barely out of place. I take in a deep breath that's supposed to be calming.

Mediating tough conflicts is usually my strong suit. But it's not exactly my arena to negotiate with badly maintained shelving.

My day hasn't been great, admittedly, but this is pissing me off. There's no reason anyone should be jamming the drawers closed this tight. This is ridiculous. I'm about to get the label maker and stick 'Janice's drawer, DO NOT FUCK WITH' on this, just so people will stop slamming it closed and making this more difficult than it has to be.

I take in another not-nearly-calming-enough breath that makes my nostrils flare.

No, I'm not going to do any of that.

I'm going to go back to my desk and write up an email reminding people about policies regarding damage to company property, and send it out to everyone on this floor and anyone I suspect may have used this cabinet. Then I'm going to send out a company-wide reminder that performance reviews are just around the corner, so that the emails show up next to each other, and it makes someone sweat.

I'm going to cast a shadow of unease over anyone who even dares think about using my drawer.

That course of action, however petty, does un-ruffle my metaphorical feathers.

I give up on trying to pull it open, but I slap the filing cabinet for good measure, one final release of aggression.

The IT department has asked me to stop slapping my computer when it gives me trouble, but for inanimate objects, I've always found percussive maintenance to be the most persuasive. I can't exactly Bcc furniture into submission.

I do glance around real quick to make sure no one saw that completely unprofessional little outburst, though. The door is open, but I–

"Do you need, uh, help there?"

I turn around completely at the voice, straightening my appearance, all the little things that I'm constantly rearranging back into place – hair, shirt, glasses. I don't usually let anyone see me as less than composed. It's important to be a little detached when you work in HR. If you let the little things get to you, or take other people's problems personally, you're going to have a bad day every day.

Luckily for me, the voice doesn't belong to anyone I recognize.

Neither does the nearly ten foot tall shadow that overtakes the doorway.

The thick black frames on his face compete for attention with the ivory tusks protruding a few inches from his lower jaw. He takes up just about the entire doorway, his shoulders wider than the frame. He's stooping through it to avoid knocking his head on the top, and a curtain of dark hair falls forward.

He kind of hunches in on himself as he steps fully inside, trying not to bump into anything. That's a task in itself just based on how he makes the storage room feel much smaller than it already is. With how he keeps his gaze to the floor though, I can't help but wonder if there's a self-conscious element in the action.

I can see that the right side of his head is shaved to the scalp, in typical Orc fashion, revealing a pointed and torn up ear, a number of sharp looking piercings through it.

My eyes draw down his button up shirt, the way the fabric strains at those poor little buttons whenever he breathes in. The pocket protector on the left side of his shirt is wide enough to hold four different colored pens and a calculator.

He must be from accounting or something.

"It's stuck," I say, nodding my head to the cabinet. I spare a glance at his arms, which are probably about as wide as one of my thighs, if I had to guess. I know Orcs are big-boned, but I imagine there's enough muscle there for him to pry the cabinet open.

"Probably because of that dent in it," he nods, talking more to my shoes than to me. Now that he mentions it, I spot a little dent in the bottom corner. "May I?"

I nod, and shuffle around him in the tiny room to let him at the corner filing cabinet.

He kneels before it, about eye level with the stuck drawer, and gives it a tug.

Nothing.

At first, I think it's because his fingers are a little too large to get a proper hold on the little drawer handle. The second time he tugs however, the whole filing cabinet shifts forward a couple inches out of its indents in the carpet.

"No, you gotta sort-of-angle-upwards when you pull," I say, crossing over and gripping what space is left for me on the handle.

I don't know what it is in me, I just can't stand by and watch a job be done incorrectly.

I yank sort-of-upwards, once, twice—

The drawer springs free, and my elbow flies back, colliding with his nose.

He falls back, and my hands cover my mouth, downgrading my shriek of horror to a squeak.

"Oh no, I'm so sorry—" I start to say, my face turning scarlet. The mortification spreads through my body from there, heat moving through me like ink in water.

I just elbowed his face. Did I break something? Surely Orc bones are too solid for a puny human to shatter, right?

"Don't worry, it was just an accident," he says, his massive hand cupped over his nose protectively, like I might do more damage than I already have.

"But your nose, I am so sorry," I repeat like it'll do anything.

He waves his other hand to dismiss my concern and shrugs casually like being elbowed in the face is nothing to be concerned over, and not something we need to file a whole accident report over.

He removes his hand and dark green blood is dripping down his face. Some of it is smeared on his palm, and his eyes darken behind his glasses when he looks at it. "Oh, fuck."

I gasp at the sight of what I've done, and as soon as I breathe in, all the hair on my skin stands up, a storm of red flushing my cheeks.

My heart is pounding and my head feels a little funny. Not like I'm going to faint at the sight of blood or anything like that, but more like the fog of a fever taking over. It's not just my forehead, I can feel it all the way down my stomach.

"Yeah, uh, that's what I'm saying, it's bad," I tell him. I turn away, searching the room for a tissue box, but the feeling continues to bloom. There's a package of paper towels stored here, for the office kitchen. I tear through the plastic and haphazardly rip a few off.

When I turn back around, the feeling returns in a second wave. It's so heavy I think I forget to breathe for a solid few seconds. It's definitely too hot in this room for me to be wearing this cardigan.

I look at him, tipping his head back, trying to pinch the bridge of his nose gingerly with one hand and cupping the other beneath his chin to catch the blood. A drop has already stained his shirt, the fabric straining even more intensely at the buttons than it was before.

"You're supposed to lean your head forward for a nosebleed," I mumble. The words don't come out the way I want them to, authoritative, like I've got this, like I'm keeping my cool in bad situations. "Something about gravity and… oh."

My knees feel weak as I try to move closer to hand him the paper towels. They fall out of my hand, drifting pathetically down onto his lap. I don't even have the capability to cringe at myself for dropping them, I'm so physically overwhelmed, and I have no idea why.

It's then I recognize some of the sensations sweeping through my body. The desperate, aching hollow between my legs, the pulsing arousal of my clit, the fact that I can tell exactly where my nipples are in my bra now.

My blood shouldn't be rushing anywhere but my brain in this situation.

I need to get out of this room.

I turn around and stuff my reports in the drawer, before running out the door. I don't know what's come over me, but I can barely think until I'm in the bathroom near my office, pressing my face against the cold porcelain of the sink. I turn on the tap and only barely resist sticking my entire head underneath it like a woman in a badly written 90's movie. Instead I'm at least a little more mindful of my makeup. I cup cold handfuls of water to my cheeks and forehead and avoid making my mascara run.

The air in here is cool and easy. I gulp down breaths like I'd just been drowning.

When I have a little bit of my brain back, I yank a dozen paper towels out of the dispenser and soak them under the tap. I wring them out and press them to my neck. For the first time in ten minutes, I can think like a person that has manners and is considerate of others.

I was just super rude to that Orc from accounting.

"Fuck," I groan. I really just elbowed him in the face, threw some paper towels at him and left. I definitely didn't put my papers in the right spot in that drawer either.

I need to go back and apologize for all of that. He'd tried to help me, and I'd essentially beat him up.

That makes me snort a little. I wonder if there's ever been an HR complaint filed for a human knocking an Orc on his ass before.

My laugh turns into a hiccup, and then a dizzy feeling. I don't understand it. I've never gotten sick from seeing blood before.

Maybe sick isn't the right word for it. None of that was necessarily a bad feeling, just entirely inappropriate.

Even thinking about it makes me feel feverish and my heart pound.

I do not have enough PTO to deal with this.

If you enjoyed this book, you can find updates on future projects, events, content notes, and subscribe to the author's sporadic newsletter at kate-prior.com.

You can follow Kate on socials: Instagram, Threads, or Tiktok @bykateprior, or join her reader's group on Facebook, *Kate's Priory of Paranormal Romance*.

If you enjoy learning about the craft of writing or finding solidarity in the ups and downs of publishing, listen to the podcast *Romance Writer's Therapy*, hosted by Kate Prior and Marty Vee.

More by Kate Prior

Mated to My Ex (Hayes Brothers 1)

He's her ex-husband. She's his fated mate.

Elise always knew she would run into her ex-husband again, eventually. What she didn't expect was that he would show up in the community she's built for herself and reveal that the family she's been working for is the same family that disapproved of their marriage eight years ago and refused to meet her. Now he's back in town for his brother's wedding, the very same one she's catering.

Shawn's always known that marrying a human went against his pack's rules. It's bad enough that she's become deeply entrenched in his hometown, but when he senses his mate is somewhere nearby, he knows he's in trouble.

It just can't be his ex-wife. If she was his true mate, he would have knotted in her eight years ago.

The Orc from the Office (Claws & Cubicles 2)

Mate-bonding with a co-worker is against company policy... accidentally or not. Janice knows better than anyone that entanglements with co-workers are risky business.
But when Janice accidentally breaks a co-workers nose, she finds herself unexpectedly mated to an orc, and under Monster Resources' scrutiny. Khent from the IT Department is quiet and nerdy, despite the tusks. His emails are overly wordy. He won't stop apologizing even though she's the one who broke his glasses. Clearly, fate got this one wrong.
All Janice has to do is stay away from Khent until the bond dissipates. Easy enough, right? Except...

...Her company laptop chooses this week to need the orc from the IT Department, repeatedly.

...She accidentally clicks on orc porn at work and has to take remedial phishing training with Khent.

...Their bond will keep pulling them back together until it is completed.

A siren in heat, a gargoyle who keeps getting under her skin, and an inescapable work trip…

Gwen doesn't want anyone to know she's a siren. She doesn't want anyone to know she's terrible at her job either.

Perhaps least on her list of priorities, Gwen would also like to avoid the gargoyle who saw her vibrator in the TSA check. Except, the very same gargoyle is the new manager she has to work with, and he's going to the same corporate retreat she is. He reminds her too much of her past and exactly the career-driven sort of guy she can't stand from Fortune 666 companies.

When things start to heat up between them, Gwen's afraid he's going to learn all her secrets, but when he offers to help feed her siren appetite, she can't resist mixing business with pleasure.

When Diane faints during her wedding vows, it's expected. Her family thinks almost everything is too stimulating for her because of her fainting condition. Of course they matched her with a man who couldn't make anyone's heart flutter.

When her fiancé tries to make light of the situation by giving her a fainting goat, the ridicule is too much to bear.

Diane wants more than the life before her— she wants to live the passion and adventure she's only ever found in the erotic sketches she creates, and the kind of heart-racing feelings her fiancé's cousin and best man Liam gives her.

The last thing Diane expects as she flees from the church, however, is for the best man to run away with her.

And They Were Broommates
(A short story included in Hexes and Ohs: A Witch
Paranormal Romance Collection for Charity)
Astrid is breaking her lease. The tower isn't big enough
for her and Jason, and the town only needs one resident witch.
She's tired of competing with him over every little thing.

Except, the lease-breaking ritual goes wrong, and they
end up with a strange bond letting them hear everything the
other is thinking. They didn't need a psychic link to know they
hated each other, but now they can't hide everything else they
think about each other.

Only One Bedroll
(A short story included in Snow, Lights, and Monster Nights,
a Romance Collection for Charity)
Mushrooms, halfling-eating monsters, and orcs, oh my.
When Bianca Chanterelle gets lost in the woods, she doesn't
expect the orc hunter that finds her to be any help getting back
to her traveling party, but with him finds adventure, a secret
microbiome, a terrifying monster, and a budding attraction
between them.

Tanis, son of Dhane the Bloodthirsty, shouldn't be so
curious about the halfling woman who is utterly unsuited to
living in the woods, but he can't resist the way his blood calls
to her, especially when they find themselves hiding in a tent,
sharing his bedroll.

When the rest of the orcish hunting party decides to raid
the traveling halfling troupe of actors, however, a staged
kidnapping and a monster intervention may not be enough to
make sure everyone gets out of the woods.

www.ingramcontent.com/pod-product-compliance
Lightning Source LLC
Chambersburg PA
CBHW061246140726
47998CB00006B/2111